THE CASE OF A BEAGLE AND A BODY

CURLY BAY ANIMAL RESCUE COZY MYSTERY BOOK 5

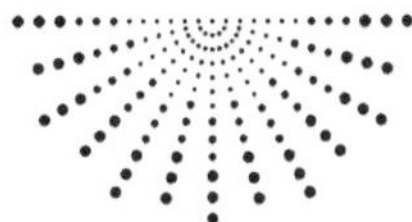

DONNA DOYLE

PUREREAD.COM

CONTENTS

Chapter 1   1
Chapter 2   11
Chapter 3   19
Chapter 4   29
Chapter 5   41
Chapter 6   52
Chapter 7   63
Chapter 8   72
Chapter 9   87
Chapter 10   98

Other books in this series   107
Our Gift To You   109

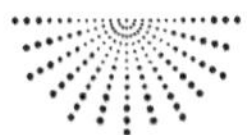

"Come on, Peppa. It's all right, sugar. I promise, nobody is going to hurt you." Courtney Cain felt her blood pressure rising as she held out a treat for the little beagle mix, who only continued to press herself into the furthest corner of her cage at the Curly Bay Pet Hotel and Rescue. Courtney wasn't mad. She was just frustrated. Some of the animals who came into the shelter had been through some trauma, which made it difficult for them to trust people again. Unfortunately, that also meant it was very difficult to get them adopted out.

"Jessi, have you had any luck with her?"

Jessi, the employee who specialized in the shelter side of things, was scooping dog food out of a big bin in preparation for the dogs' dinner. Her brow was wrinkled under her fringe of short hair, and her big earrings flashed in the fluorescent lights, but she said nothing.

"Jessi?"

"Hm? Oh, sorry. Were you talking to me?" Jessi paused in her portioning, but she didn't have the same light in her eyes that she normally did when she was dealing with the animals. Jessi had already been employed by the shelter when Courtney came to work there, but one of the things Courtney had noticed about her right away was her genuine concern for the wellbeing of the animals. She wasn't just there because she got paid, and she always carried out her work with a surprising amount of energy.

"I was. Are you all right?" Courtney set the dog treat down in the front of the cage, giving Peppa a chance to come get it without having to get near a human hand. She knew the treat would remain where it was until long after all the humans had cleared the room.

"Sure. I'm fine. What did you need?" Jessi took her cell phone out of her back pocket, frowned at the screen, and then put it back again.

There was obviously something going on, but if she wasn't interested in talking about it, Courtney wasn't going to force her. Everyone had a bad day now and then. "I was just wondering if you've been having any luck with Peppa. The poor thing is just terrified no matter what I do." She was pretending not to look at the dog, glancing at her only from the side of her eyes, but the treat remained untouched.

Jessi sighed. "No, I can't say that I have. I've tried a few things, mostly buttering her up with treats and a lot of quiet talking. I think she's one of those that's going to need a lot more time."

"I know. A family came in the other day looking for a dog like her, but since Peppa is still so shy she wouldn't even come out to meet them. It's just as well, since they had some little kids. That might not have worked well for a dog like her." Courtney chewed her lip as she studied the pup. Peppa had been dropped off by a couple who claimed they couldn't keep her because they were moving. Perhaps it was simply being put in a shelter that'd made the beagle mix so scared, but Courtney would never really know if there was more to the story. Sometimes, she'd come to find out, it was better not to know.

"She'd probably do a lot better in the foster program," Jessi said with a sigh as she began opening cages and listlessly distributing kibble. "You know, something that isn't a chain link cage."

Courtney's heart shattered, knowing Jessi was right. They did their best to give these poor strays the best life possible, but any kind of shelter life still wasn't as good as being in a home. "I'd have to find someone willing to take her, first. We had so many people who signed up for the foster program and took dogs and cats, but now they're full. I'll have to go through the list again." Leaving the treat in case Peppa decided she wanted it, Courtney headed to her office.

She tapped her pen against her chin as she looked through the list she'd recently typed up in a spreadsheet. So many people in Curly Bay had opened up their hearts and their homes to help animals when there just wasn't enough room at the shelter. It was more than she'd ever expected, and their classes and informational sessions had only made it that much more successful. In some cases, having the chance to have these pets inside their homes made the foster parents realize just how much they loved them, and quite a few cats and dogs had ended up with a permanent place.

But a bubble of guilt was living in Courtney's heart because she herself couldn't participate. She cared for these creatures as though they were her own, and she managed the entire facility with the pets' needs at the forefront, but her landlord didn't allow animals. Courtney had once brought home a German shepherd whose owner had passed away. It was just for one night, since the poor dog was so miserable in the kennel, but Mrs. Peabody had been livid.

Maybe it was time to finally buy a home. Courtney hadn't been certain what her future would hold when she'd come to Curly Bay, and she'd rented an apartment just in case this new job didn't work out. But she'd been there for several months now, and there was no way she was leaving when so many cats and dogs still needed her. She was staying, and it was time to settle down permanently.

She was just looking up the number of a real estate agent she'd met a few months ago when the bell over the front door told her a customer had come in. Courtney stepped up to the front desk to help, knowing Jessi was busy with feeding and Dora was likely grooming.

A woman with stick-straight strawberry blonde hair and a thin frame was standing at the counter. She frowned slightly, her hands clenching the end of a pink leash with crystal studs. At the other end of that leash danced a Boston terrier who was thrilled at all the new scents.

"Hi. What can I do for you?" Courtney asked with a friendly smile. She could tell right away by the couture outfit and the way she carried herself this woman wasn't interested in getting dirty with a bunch of strays.

"My name is Rachel DuBois," she said, her voice far sterner than her small frame denoted. "I'm going on vacation, and I need a place to leave my Maggie."

"Oh, that's nice!" Courtney enthused. "Where are you going?"

Raquel's frown deepened. "Cancun, if you must know."

Usually, clients were more than happy to talk about their travel destinations and sometimes even liked to brag about how much money they were spending. Clearly, Raquel wasn't one of them. Courtney cleared her throat. "I see. What dates are you looking at? I'll check the calendar to see if we're available."

The woman's lips drew even more tightly together. "I'm not sure that's worth it if I don't know whether or not I even *want* to leave my Maggie here. I've looked at another kennel or two, and they simply aren't up to par."

"I can assure you, we're the best place in Curly Bay. We've got every amenity you can imagine for Maggie, from massage to nail polish to mud masks."

"I wouldn't even dream of saying yes without taking a tour," Raquel sniffed, glancing around the lobby as though she expected to find something horrific just over her shoulder.

Courtney glanced at the clock. She still had to get payroll done for the week, order supplies, and take a couple of cats to Dr. Moulton's office for their shots. "I could do a short one. Right this way, please."

She brought Raquel and Maggie over to the right side of the office, where the pet hotel and day spa was located. Ms. O'Donnell, the owner of the business, had explained to Courtney that the ritzier side of things had been created in order to fund the shelter side. It was a brilliant plan, although Courtney was often surprised by what different lives these animals had from one side of the building to the other.

"You can see that each pet has his or her own cage, and that they're completely separated by solid walls.

This helps with any animals who have problems playing well with others. Dora here does all of our grooming, and she's an expert in numerous different haircuts and techniques."

Dora, who had no idea the tour was going to happen, simply nodded and smiled and continued her work on a Shih Tzu.

A loud ringing filled the room, and Raquel was looking through her purse. She made no effort to excuse herself or apologize as she took out her cell and answered it. "What is it, Aaron?" Her expression grew even more sour as she listened. "No, I don't. I already told you that. It's my money and I'll do what I want to with it." Another pause. "Yes, including that! It isn't really any of your business, now is it?" She huffed and closed her eyes, pinching the bridge of her nose with one hand. "I'm not going over this with you again. Goodbye." She hung up, put her phone away, and gestured impatiently for Courtney to continue as though it was her fault the tour had been interrupted.

Courtney pointed out the tag on one of the occupied cages. "You can see here that we print out a new tag for every guest with their name and their needs. This can include what and when to feed them as well as any extra services you'd like to pay for while they're here. That includes the spa options as well as supervised playtime or snuggle sessions." Courtney had found that plenty of people who were already shelling out the big bucks for an elite doggie hotel would also gladly hand over a few extra dollars just to make sure their dog or cat got some extra loving during the day.

"I see," was Raquel's simple answer.

Courtney looked around, quite proud of the place. The wealthiest people in Curly Bay entrusted them with their furbabies, and she couldn't imagine a better place for a pampered pet to stay. "Do you have any questions about anything?"

Maggie stretched out to the very end of her leash to sniff Dora's pant leg, her stumpy tail wagging as she tipped her head back to beg for attention.

"No, I don't think I do. We won't be needing your services, thank you." Raquel turned on her heel, yanking the leash to get Maggie away from Dora.

Courtney stood confused for a moment before following her back to the front. "I'm sorry. Is there a problem?"

Raquel shook her pinkish locks over her shoulder as she tipped up her chin. "This place simply isn't good enough for my baby."

While Courtney really didn't want to have to deal with a woman that snobby, she couldn't help but be insulted. "We're not only the best place in town, but the only place that offers such specialized services. You'd have to go into a larger city to find anything even comparable."

"Then I'll do just that. Come *on,* Maggie!"

The Boston had stopped to sniff at a pallet of dog food bags that had recently been delivered but not put up yet. She stopped at the command of her owner and trotted out the door.

"Well, no loss there," Dora commented, coming into the foyer.

"I guess not." Courtney squinted out the front glass doors, watching as Raquel got into her car. Courtney had expected a BMW or a Mercedes to be waiting on her, so the rather conservative Toyota made her wonder just what this woman's deal was. "I feel kind of sorry for Maggie, though. They say dogs are like their owners, but I don't think that's the case for them."

CHAPTER TWO

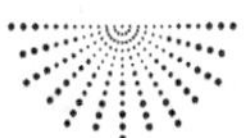

On Saturday morning, when Courtney had the day off, she stepped into the office of Carolyn Cheatham. Carolyn's estranged—and now late—husband had been killed a few months ago, and Courtney had met her in the process of finding a new home for his dog. It had been that German shepherd Courtney had tried to bring home, in fact, which Courtney thought was kind of ironic.

Carolyn got up from behind her large oak desk and came around to shake Courtney's hand. While Courtney had seen plenty of realtors go casual these days, Carolyn was always dressed to the nines. The emerald green pantsuit set off her short red hair that had been curled into a carefree style as well as her brilliant red lipstick. "Courtney, it's so very nice to see you again! Have a seat, and we can go over a few things before we get started. I have a few places in mind that I'd like to show you, but I need to know a little bit more about what you want out of a house."

She sounded so excited as she spoke, like they were getting ready to do something much more than just look at a few buildings, and it made the ball of nervous energy in Courtney's stomach expand. "It doesn't have to be anything huge, since it's just me. I would like to have some yard space, though. The shelter has a foster program, and I'd like a chance to participate in it instead of just watching everyone else do so." Courtney thought wistfully of Peppa, who was still so uncertain.

"I see. And your budget?"

Courtney told her, and Carolyn made a note. "Right. Okay. Some of the places I show you today probably won't be exactly what you want, but I think it's important to explore the town and really see what's out there. Sometimes you don't know what you want until you see it. We'll take my car." She beamed as she escorted Courtney out to her sleek sedan.

Courtney whistled when they pulled up to the first house and she craned her head to glance up through the windshield at the brick two-story. "Um, how much is this place?"

"Uh uh," Carolyn said with a smile and her finger in the air. "Everyone gets too focused on budget to think about what they actually want. That's what I specialize in, Courtney. I want people to really be happy, to really connect to a house. We won't talk about price until you've seen it. It won't kill either one of us if you look at a few houses that are outside your price range or your needs, because then you'll know at least you looked." She eagerly hopped out of the car and strode toward the front door.

Courtney kept having to press her lips shut as they admired the hardwood floors, corner fireplace, and newly remodeled kitchen.

"Now, without thinking about the price at all, tell me what you love and hate about this house." Carolyn couldn't stop smiling. With her pert nose and catlike eyes, she always looked as though she knew more than everyone else around her.

"It's beautiful," Courtney admitted, trying really hard not to think about how much the owners were asking. "I'm concerned that it's too big for just me, and I don't think hardwood floors are a good idea if I'm going to have dogs running around."

"Fair enough. On to the next!"

Courtney realized she was expecting Carolyn to be upset about taking up her time on a house she wasn't going to buy. After all, realtors got paid for each sale, not for each showing. But Carolyn happily drove through town to one house after the next, listening carefully every time she invited Courtney to speak her true feelings about what they'd just looked at. Courtney realized Carolyn truly meant it when she wanted a buyer to have a real connection to the home.

"Now this one is a bit of a fixer upper, but it has a huge backyard that's already fenced." Carolyn had pulled up in front of a small bungalow.

Courtney thought they were in the driveway, but it was impossible to tell with all the weeds that had grown up in front of it. The front door wasn't even a door but a large piece of plywood that'd been screwed into place. "How are we supposed to get in?"

"Don't worry," Carolyn said with a dazzling smile, as though they weren't sitting in front of a place that looked like it should be a haunted house instead of a possible residence. "Realtors always have a way!" She brought Courtney around to the back of the house, where there was still a functioning door.

Courtney pulled her shirt up over her nose. "I sure hope nobody is living here." The place smelled of mold and mildew. The hardwood floors didn't have even the thinnest coat of varnish left on them anymore. The walls were done in old, cheap paneling that'd gone wavy with moisture.

"There isn't a fence in the back, but it's a very large yard. It wouldn't take much to cut down the excess weeds and bushes. Inside, you'd have free reign to do what you want as far as remodeling, since all the cabinets would need to come out," Carolyn offered brightly.

"I'd say so." Courtney gave the house the fairest chance she could by going ahead and looking through each room, but she knew this wasn't going to work for her. "I don't think there's anything I love about this house," she said before the realtor had a chance to ask, "but I definitely can't take anything that needs this much work. I don't have the time or the skills to work on it, and it'll cost a lot to hire someone."

Carolyn nodded. "I understand. Honestly, the price is the one thing there is to love when it comes to this house." She rattled off the price.

"That's cheaper than the last car I bought by half!" Courtney said with a laugh.

"Moving on!" Carolyn locked up and they were back in the car.

Easily navigating through town, Carolyn didn't even have to check a map or a phone to find the place she was looking for. "This bungalow was built in 1916," she explained as they stepped under the covered front porch. "It's been remodeled, but with the idea of keeping a lot of the original charm."

Inside, Courtney found striped and floral wallpaper, formal furniture on hunter green carpet, and another newly remodeled kitchen. There were two bedrooms upstairs, with room for an additional space if she wanted to finish it off. The backyard wasn't huge, but it already had a solid privacy fence. The house had an interesting energy about it that Courtney liked.

"I see that look in your eyes," Carolyn said. "Talk to me."

"It's pretty great, honestly. I like that it's got some historic value, but it isn't as though it's too nice to have some cats or dogs in here. The yard's not bad. I think you know what I'm waiting for."

Carolyn nodded. "It's right in the middle of that first house and the fixer-upper. I can vouch for the neighborhood, though. I know the Andersons across the street." She pointed through the window to another bungalow, which seemed to be the trend in this neighborhood.

"And?" Courtney pressed.

The realtor gave her the price.

It was right on budget. The house wasn't exactly what Courtney wanted, but it was probably the closest. She'd already seen most of the homes that were for sale in Curly Bay, and they all seemed to be either far too expensive or they needed too much work. "It's a good middle ground. I'm tempted to tell you I'll take it, but I know part of that is just because I'm so ready to get out of that apartment. I'll think about it for now."

"Of course! There's never any pressure, dear. You need to do what's right for you. I still have a little bit of time if you'd like to look at a few more," Carolyn offered.

Courtney took one last look around, soaking it all in and committing it to memory. She could see herself living here, in this house that wasn't too big or too small. Still, Carolyn had been right. If she explored more, then at least she'd know she looked at everything. "Yeah, let's do that."

As they pulled out of the driveway, Courtney felt as though she were leaving something behind. She wasn't. She had her cell and her purse, but it wasn't anything physical. She turned around to get another look at the place. "What about the neighbors next door?" she asked impulsively, eyeing the small Victorian next door. It was painted a pale blue with white trim, and it shared a fence line with Courtney's potential new home. "Do you know them?"

"I can't say that I do." They headed on to look at a few other places while Courtney mulled over the difficulty of making such a big life decision.

"Sorry I'm late," Courtney said as she slid into the booth across from Lisa at Salazar's Salad Bar and immediately snagged one of the light, fluffy rolls that were kept freshly stocked on every table. "I'm absolutely starving, though. I guess I wasn't thinking of house hunting as being such hard work."

Lisa, who worked at the local library and had adopted both a dog and a cat from the Curly Bay Pet Hotel and Rescue, nodded sagely. "I hear that. When I moved to town, it was so hard to make a decision. If you can imagine a type of house, you'll probably find it here. Did you settle on anything?"

"Maybe." After Courtney ordered a bowl of soup, the two of them made a trip to the salad bar. Courtney piled a bowl full of greens as she described the house. "It's actually a lot cuter than I thought I could afford. There are a lot of little things it had, simply because it's so old, that I didn't see in the other homes, like solid wood doors with crystal knobs. Whoever updated it tried to keep some of that old charm."

"Just beware of what lies underneath that old charm," Lisa warned as she used a pair of tongs to pluck a few cherry tomatoes out of the bin and put on her salad. "There's a gentleman who comes into the library a lot who sometimes flips houses. He's told me there have been several times when he's seen someone make a house look good to the naked eye without going through and fixing the plumbing and electrical. That could cost you a lot of money if you don't know what you're getting into."

"That's true," Courtney admitted. "Carolyn advised me to get a home inspection on anything I'm serious about, and I'll do it."

"Good. We have a few people on file at the library if you need any help finding someone. What about the noise level in the neighborhood?" Lisa added a couple of croutons.

Courtney frowned at the selection of salad dressing before she plucked the bottle of vinaigrette from its holder. "I don't really know. I don't remember hearing anything out of the ordinary while I was there. Or at any of the other houses, for that matter."

"I wish I'd gone back to my place several different times before I actually bought it," Lisa lamented as they headed back to the table. "I had no idea how well I'd be able to hear the train come through. Someone had told me to do that, but I didn't listen."

"Wow," Courtney said as they sat back down. "There's a lot more to think about than just the size of the back yard and the mortgage payment. It's kind of a bummer."

"I'm sorry. I wasn't trying to be a downer. It's just that a house is a really big commitment, and I don't want you to be unhappy. Oh, if the house is that old, the historical society might have some information on it, too."

"Right, like someone died of the Spanish flu there and was buried in the backyard?" Courtney asked with an ironic smile.

"Well, I guess you never know! I was thinking more along the lines of someone famous being born there, or just finding out more about the property itself.

I'm sorry. I just love to research, and I wish I'd done more of it on my place." She raised her eyebrows and gave her friend a sad look. "Can you forgive me for being such a bummer?"

"Oh, of course! I'm not upset. I just got so excited about buying a place, and it's turning out to be a lot more work and a lot more decisions than I realized. And I haven't even moved yet! I think you're right, though. Nobody's living the house, so I can go back a few times and just check it out. Maybe I'll walk around the neighborhood a little bit."

"I think that's a great idea," Lisa agreed. "I'll even go with you if you want."

"You would? It would be so nice to get a second opinion." Courtney sliced a rather large cucumber that'd ended up in her salad, suddenly feeling much better about the whole thing. The only people she knew in Curly Bay other than Lisa were either coworkers or clients of the pet hotel. She didn't mind being on her own, but it was still nice to know she had someone else looking out for her best interests.

The waitress arrived just then with their orders. "I've got one bowl of Spanish rice soup, and one of chicken tortilla. Be careful, because they're super hot. Do you ladies need any crackers or anything?" She stood at the end of the table with her eyebrows raised and a pleasant smile on her face, clearly more than happy to get them anything they needed. Courtney and Lisa told her they were fine, and the waitress moved on.

"You know, that's one of the reasons I love coming here. Other than the rolls, I mean."

"What's that?" Lisa gleefully crumbled tortilla chips into her soup.

"The service. It's just a little soup-and-sandwich place, and given that half of the menu is over there on the salad bar, they don't really need to have great wait staff. Yet every time we come here, they act like we're long-lost cousins that've just flown into town. I love it."

Lisa had turned to look across the dining room, frowning. "I guess not everyone feels that way."

Their waitress was standing at the end of a couple's table, just as she'd been at their own a moment ago. Courtney could only see the back of the man's head, but she recognized the woman across from them as Raquel DuBois. Even without her adorable dog, she was hard to miss with that strawberry blonde hair and angry face. It was easy to hear the conversation, given how quiet the restaurant was at that hour.

"How can you seriously not have squash soup? It's the only reason I come to this dump in the first place!" Raquel slapped her hand on the table for emphasis.

"I'm sorry," the waitress said, obviously working hard to keep her patience. "It's just been very popular this week with the weather getting colder. Can I offer you some New England clam chowder? Or our quinoa chicken parmesan soup?"

"Ech!" Raquel flicked her manicured fingers as she made a noise of absolute disgust. "How can you even suggest any of those? Just go in the back and check again. You have squash soup every time I come in here, and that's what I want."

The waitress took a deep breath, her cheeks reddening. Courtney waited for her to explode and tell Raquel just where she could get off, but instead she turned from the table and marched back to the kitchen.

"Wow," Lisa whispered, rolling her eyes. "Some customers are just impossible to please."

Courtney nodded. "I know! That same woman came into work the other day, and she said we weren't good enough to watch her dog!"

"That's laughable. I'd like to see her find someone better."

"I guess I would, too. If she doesn't come crawling back to us, then someone else will have to deal with her." If this was how Raquel DuBois dealt with everyone she encountered, then it was a shock anyone in Curly Bay would still do business with her.

The soup and salad were delicious, and the two ladies tucked in. Courtney didn't think of herself as a nosy person, but she found it impossible not to eavesdrop on the conversation happening on the other side of the room. Raquel didn't make it any easier, since she was so loud.

"Don't let it bother you, sweetie," her companion said sweetly as he reached across the table to pat her hand. He was a large man, and his hand covered hers completely. "I'm sure we can find your soup somewhere else. Or maybe I can look up a recipe and make some for you."

Raquel wasn't so easily consoled. "I guess," she sneered, "but it just won't be the same. They do it perfectly here, otherwise I'd never let myself be seen in a place like this."

"Come on, now. A salad bar isn't really that bad of a place, is it?" The man spoke with a smooth, even tone, like he was trying to calm a horse.

"Whatever. Let's just talk about our vacation instead. I can't wait to get out of Curly Bay. I don't want to see all this low-class trash around me anymore." Raquel stabbed her fork violently into her salad.

"Cancun is going to be an absolute blast," he replied, running a hand through his sandy blonde hair. "We'll have all that sun and sand to soak up, and we won't know anybody there. It'll be perfect."

"I guess, but I'd much rather go someplace more exotic. Saint-Tropez. Monaco. You know, anything that has to do with the French Riviera. I know you can afford it, Jordan. You were just saying you're due for a promotion."

Her companion rubbed the thighs of his pants anxiously. "I think we have different definitions of what it means to afford something, sweetheart. I technically do have the money, but it's tied up in investments. That money is going to mean I'll have a nice retirement someday."

Raquel gave an impatient sigh. "Someday? But what about living right now? I swear, I thought you were different. Everyone is too tied up with being practical. It's ridiculous. For once in my life, I'd just like to go on a nice vacation without having to think about it so darn much." She folded her arms across her chest and glared out the window.

"You know," Lisa said slowly as she swirled her spoon in her soup, "I didn't realize we'd get free entertainment with this meal. I'll have to give the waitress a bigger tip than I planned."

Trying not to laugh too loudly, Courtney spied the waitress come back out of the kitchen. She carried a bowl in her hand, her thumb over the rim, and slapped it on the table. "That's the closest I can get. Have a nice day." She turned and stormed back into the kitchen before giving Raquel a chance to reply.

Courtney had tried not to stare directly at the couple to avoid being noticed, but now it was just impossible. She watched as Raquel peered into the bowl, sniffed it, and shoved it across the table. Orangey liquid sloshed out and onto the table, some of it splattering onto her dining companion's shirt. "I don't know what that is, but I'm not eating it!"

He dipped a finger into the bowl and licked it. "Tomato."

Courtney shook her head and finished her meal, grateful for being single and not having to worry about any of their problems.

"Okay. It's been a whole day. Are you still thinking about the same house?" Lisa asked from the passenger seat.

It was Sunday afternoon. The library was closed. The shelter was only open by appointment, and Courtney had already run in to make sure all the pets were fed, watered, and walked. Jessi would take the evening shift on feeding, so she was free for the rest of the day. "I am. I sat down last night with a big sheet of paper and made a big table with all the information about all the houses Carolyn and I looked at. The addresses, how many bedrooms, how many baths, the price, the pros, the cons, everything I could think of. The one that still fit the bill was this particular house."

"That sounds like progress, then," Lisa said as she sat back against the seat and looked out the window. "I just love this time of year. The leaves are starting to fall, the mornings are cool, and we get a lot more cloudy days. Those are my favorite for being at the library, since it's such good reading weather."

Courtney held up a finger. "Just as long as the rain doesn't keep me from moving. Now that I've had a chance to look at some houses and it's starting to feel real, I almost can't stand being in my apartment right now."

"I was wondering why you were in such a rush. The last time we'd talked about it, you weren't sure you were ready to buy yet," Lisa noted.

"I know," Courtney said with a sigh. "You see, I started feeling guilty as soon as the foster program began. There I was, standing in front of a whole room full of people at the Old Train Depot, telling them everything they needed to know to be able to take in a foster dog or cat. But I couldn't do it. I'm certainly qualified, but because I rent it just wasn't possible."

"You can't beat yourself up too much over that," Lisa advised. "You already spend all day taking care of those animals and finding them homes. I know you care, but is it really such a bad thing if you get a break every now and then?"

Courtney laughed lightly. "Technically, no, but it is kind of addictive. When I first came to Curly Bay, having worked in an executive office focused on marketing, I wasn't sure I'd enjoy this job. Now, I don't know what to do with myself if I'm not grooming or cleaning or feeding or scooping. It's just part of who I am now. Here we are." She slowed down as she turned onto the next road. "I want you to do me a favor."

"Of course."

"Be honest with me. I'm sure there are things I'm missing just because I'm excited about the house, so if there's anything you see or hear or sense, just let me know. I don't care if it's a cobweb that you don't like the look of, just let me know. I need as unbiased an opinion as possible."

Lisa lightly tapped Courtney's arm. "You're thinking about this too much, and it's all my fault! I put all those ideas in your head about making sure you had the perfect place. In all honesty, Courtney, nothing is going to be perfect."

"You don't think I should strive to find something that's at least as close to perfect as possible?"

Courtney challenged, the corner of her mouth tweaking up.

"I guess we'll just have to look at it and find out, and then I'll let you know," Lisa replied with a giggle.

"You've got your chance, because here we are." Courtney pulled in the driveway, put the car in park, and shut off the engine. "Even seeing it the next day, I think I still like it."

"Oh, that's cute!" Lisa unbuckled her seatbelt as they pulled in the driveway. "The porch could use a coat of paint, but it looks like it's in really good shape. I'm no home inspector, of course."

"We can walk around to the back if you'd like."

"Sure."

The gate to the privacy fence had been left open, so they went around the back corner to explore the yard. The moist dirt and the leaves that'd piled up in the corners of the fence carried the scent of fall, and Courtney eyed the back porch. "This is a little smaller than what's on the front, but it'd still be a great place to come outside and be with whatever dogs I have here. What are you smiling at?"

"That there are people in the world like you who base such a big decision almost entirely on how good it'll be for homeless animals. You've got a big heart, Courtney."

"Maybe too big," Courtney grumbled. "You see, there's this beagle mix named Peppa. She's really sweet and adorable, and I know she'd make a great pet for the right person. But she's so shy that she'll hardly even come out of her cage. Jessi pointed out how the foster program might benefit her, but I don't have anyone available to take her. It just breaks my heart knowing her life is being wasted in that cage instead of getting the help she needs."

"I see. If it helps, I'll put the word out at the library again. There were quite a few patrons who stepped up, and you never know who might be willing now."

"Thanks. I really appreciate it. In the meantime, want to walk around the neighborhood a bit?"

They got a little exercise in while they strolled around the block, looking and listening. Courtney was having a good time simply because she was with her friend and the weather was beautiful, but she could also tell this was a pretty nice place. People kept their yards picked up. There weren't any dilapidated houses or junk cars anywhere, and the street was well maintained. "I think I'm starting to have a little too much hope for this place," Courtney admitted.

"Let's stop in and talk to your future next-door neighbor," Lisa suggested, pointing at the blue Victorian.

"Do you really think it's okay?" Courtney's curiosity was strong, but she didn't want to disturb anybody.

Lisa shrugged. "My sister went back to our hometown a few years ago and found our old house. She knocked on the door and asked to come in and look around to see her childhood home. They actually let her, so I'd say stranger things have happened."

"Good enough for me, then." Courtney led the way up the little curved sidewalk that led them up to the front door. She noted the freshly painted door and the topiaries sitting on either side of it. There was hardly a fallen leaf on the lawn, and even outside the place smelled of air freshener. She pressed the doorbell, hearing the echo of it from within the confines of the house along with the barking of a small dog.

After a moment, Courtney realized the barking wasn't coming from inside the house. She turned around just in time to see the black and white blur of a Boston terrier come racing around the corner of the house. Its back legs skidded out behind it as it made the turn, but it quickly recovered and dashed up onto the porch, barking like mad.

"Whoa, hey! I know you." Courtney knelt down and held her hand out for the dog to sniff. "I recognize that pink collar."

"One of your clients?" Lisa asked, smiling in amusement as the dog's barks slowed down to a bit of a growl. It stepped forward and sniffed the proffered hand, its little stump wagging happily.

"No, not exactly. You remember that woman at Salazar's who was throwing such a fit over her soup? I'm afraid this poor creature belongs to her." Courtney scratched the dog's chin. "Hey, Maggie. Hi, sweets. Where's your owner at? Did you get away from your mommy? She doesn't strike me as the kind to just let you run off." She stood and looked around, expecting to find Raquel DuBois jogging through the neighborhood.

As soon as Courtney was back on her feet, the dog was taking off again. She hurled herself down the porch stairs, nearly slamming her own face into the concrete pathway as she misjudged the bottom step. Maggie didn't let it stop her for more than a split second as she careered around the house in the direction she'd come from.

Instinctively, Courtney took off after her. No dog should be out on their own without a leash or a fence, and especially a little one like that. "Maggie!" she called sweetly as she jogged down the stairs and into the yard, sidestepping a large planter of mums. "Maggie, come here, girl!"

But the dog had gone straight through to the backyard.

Courtney paused. The fence and house for the home were situated very similarly to the home she was considering buying. The gate faced the street, and it was halfway open. Courtney contemplated her options as she slowed down. She could shut the gate and keep the dog contained, but Courtney didn't know for sure that Maggie lived here. What if whoever owned the home found her and simply decided to keep her? On the other hand, if Courtney just strolled right into the backyard, she'd be trespassing on private property.

Lisa had just caught up with her. "What's going on?"

"I don't know. I do know that's Raquel's dog, and she didn't strike me as the kind to live anywhere but the absolute nicest neighborhood. I'm technically about to break the law, so it's up to you whether you want to come with me or not." Courtney typically thought of herself as a law-abiding citizen. She didn't really even go over the speed limit. Things were different when a dog or a cat was involved, though.

Lisa put her chin in the air. "I'm certainly not going to let you go in by yourself."

"Fair enough." Courtney reached out, wrapping her hand around the rough wood of the gate in the privacy fence. She pulled it open the rest of the way, and it swung easily enough on its hinges as she poked her head into the yard.

Someone had started putting in a swimming pool, even though it was so late in the year. The hole had been dug and someone had put yellow caution tape around it, but the pool itself hadn't yet been installed. Scanning the yard, Courtney discovered a fountain with fresh landscaping around it and a jacuzzi added onto the back porch. It was a far nicer outdoor space than the plain, open backyard she was contemplating.

"There she is!" Lisa whispered, pointing at the stairs that led up to the back door.

"Hello?" Courtney called out. She'd already rung the doorbell and hadn't gotten an answer. "Is anyone home?"

Maggie gave an answering bark of excitement, stamping her little feet on the decking.

"I'd say she wants us to come to her," Courtney noted, having learned quite a bit about dog language in the few months she'd been working at the Curly Bay Pet Hotel and Rescue. It didn't matter if a dog was purebred or not; they all had ways of communicating.

"Did this Raquel woman leave you her number? Maybe you could call her," Lisa suggested.

"I'm afraid not. She didn't even want to give me the dates she was leaving town to let me check the calendar." As Courtney slowly came up the steps, the dog retreated. "Come on, honey. I've got a leash in the car, and I can take you to a really nice place until we find your mommy."

The dog backed up a little further. Her ears were perked forward as she listened, but she wouldn't be cajoled. Maggie dashed to the other side of the patio, behind the jacuzzi, and came running back again.

"Okay, you have something to show me first? Did you hide a toy back here or something?" It was obvious to Courtney that Maggie wasn't going to even consider cooperating until she got her way, so perhaps she was more like her owner than Courtney had originally thought. Well past worrying about lawful entry, Courtney followed the dog around the side of the hot tub.

"Oh!" Courtney immediately took several steps backwards, bumping into Lisa.

Maggie wasn't showing them a tennis ball or a chew tie. Her owner lay on the deck boards in a pool of blood.

Lisa saw it, too. "Please tell me I'm not seeing what I think I'm seeing."

Bile rose in Courtney's throat as she nodded. "I don't like this part," she whispered as she reached down to touch the inside of Raquel's wrist. The skin was ice-cold, and she couldn't feel a heartbeat. "She's dead."

"What do we do?" Lisa looked around frantically.

Unfortunately—or perhaps fortunately, depending on how she wanted to look at it—this wasn't Courtney's first rodeo. She handed Lisa the keys to her car. "Go look in the backseat of my car. There should be a leash back there. I'll call the police."

"Okay." Lisa ran off to do her task, no doubt happy to get away from the body.

Courtney groaned as she fished her cell out of her pocket. She'd been curious about her potential new neighbors, but this wasn't what she'd been hoping to find.

CHAPTER FIVE

Courtney and Lisa were sitting on the front steps when they heard the sirens coming.

"I haven't even officially moved in, and I'm already making the neighborhood go downhill," Courtney commented.

"Hey, it's not your fault," Lisa argued gently. "It looks to me like she slipped while she was doing something near the hot tub."

"Let's just hope you're right. It'd be nice to have something genuinely be an accident for once. I thought this was a nice, quiet town, but I've certainly been encountering a lot more crime than I ever did when I lived in the city." Courtney could remember hearing plenty on the local news about robberies and accidents, but she'd never actually been involved in anything remotely scary until she'd moved to Curly Bay.

"Maybe it's a game of numbers. You know, there were just so many other people in the city that it never randomly happened to you. Or maybe you've just got a nose for trouble." Lisa smiled, trying to defuse the situation.

"And now I'm dragging you into it," Courtney commented.

"I suppose it doesn't hurt to have a little extra excitement in my life. Not much happens at the library, you know. I haven't come around the stacks or gone into the media room and found any dead bodies."

"Lucky you." Courtney reached down to soothe Maggie, who'd started to tremble at the wail of the sirens. Fortunately, since Courtney kept plenty of supplies in her car for an emergency, she'd also had an old blanket to wrap around the little dog to keep her warm.

Detective Fletcher was the first to get out of his car and come up the walkway. "When they put out the call and I heard it was you, I just had to come. What'd you do this time?"

Courtney detected just the smallest hint of a smile at the corner of the man's mouth. Fletcher always looked like he hadn't yet had his first cup of coffee, but he was good to work with. He listened, and he seemed interested in Courtney's opinions when she got herself into these situations.

She did her best to give him a quick run-down of what had happened, explaining how the dog had led them from the front porch around back to her owner's body. "It's right there by the jacuzzi. I can show you, if you'd like."

Detective Fletcher waved at two of the officers to go investigate instead. "I'm going to ask this because you know someone else will if I don't. Why were you here in the first place?"

Courtney sighed. "I was thinking about buying the house next door. I wanted to get a good feel for the neighborhood."

"And now?" he pressed.

"Now, I think I'll just keep adding to my down payment for a while."

Fletcher let out his version of a chuckle, which was so quiet it could easily be missed. "And this is the dog who spilled the beans."

"Yes. This is Maggie."

At the sound of her name, Maggie looked expectantly up at Courtney and then at Fletcher.

"You're a good girl, Maggie," Fletcher said calmly before looking back up at Courtney. "We've called the victim's husband, and he's on his way, but he might be a bit. Do you think you can stay and take care of the dog until he's here to pick it up?"

"Sure, I can do that. Or I can take her back to the shelter, if you'd like. I won't charge anything to board her for a bit."

Fletcher's face crumpled toward his nose as he thought about this for a minute, but he shook his head. "No, I think I'd rather have you here. Hang tight. We can probably at least get you into the house to warm up after we've looked around a bit. It's getting awfully chilly out here."

Courtney rubbed her arms, thinking he was right. It hadn't been bad while they were up and moving around, but sitting on cold steps didn't make things very comfortable. "Sure. We'll just take a walk and come back in a bit."

"That'd be fine. Don't go far." Fletcher sauntered around through the back gate.

Standing up, Courtney stretched her legs. "If you want to get home, you can take my car. I can have Detective Fletcher swing me by later to pick it up."

"No way," Lisa said as they hit the sidewalk once again. "First off, I was here when you found the body. If they find anything suspicious, I don't want to give them a reason to think I left the scene of the crime. Besides, this is exciting! I kind of want to be here for it."

"Haven't been spending enough time in the murder mystery section at the library?" Courtney teased.

"Or maybe too much," Lisa replied honestly. "I really shouldn't read any of it while I'm living alone. I go to bed thinking I'm fine, but I heard the slightest noise outside, and my imagination completely runs away with me."

They talked for a while about books as they made a large radius around the DuBois house, but Courtney couldn't keep her mind off the situation at hand. Of course, having Raquel's dog at the end of the leash certainly didn't make that very easy. "You know, I'm surprised that Raquel lived in this neighborhood."

"I know what you mean. This is a nice place, but I thought she was a little, well, snobbier than that. If she wanted to go on vacation on the French Riviera, you'd think she'd live out in the Majestic Oaks district. Or maybe not in Curly Bay at all."

"Exactly. It's obvious they must have some money, considering the jacuzzi, the swimming pool, and all that. And it's not like that house is a bad one, but it just doesn't add up."

"I guess we'll never know now."

They rounded the corner to see that a beige sedan had joined the emergency vehicles parked on the street. Fletcher was standing in the front yard, holding his phone, but he put it away when he saw her approach. "There you are. I was just about to call you. We've got the husband here, but I need to talk to him for a bit. The back door and the kitchen have been cleared, so you can come in and sit down."

"Thank you. I think Maggie will appreciate it, too." Courtney had been concerned not only for the dog's warmth, but figured she needed some food and water as well.

They once again went around the back side of the house, where Courtney felt she'd already been far too many times. She avoided looking anywhere near the hot tub and the officers and paramedics working there as they stepped in the back door.

"I'll just be in the next room, and I'll let you know when I need anything else from you." Fletcher stalked through an arched doorway.

Courtney kept Maggie on the leash so she wouldn't disturb anyone else, but she brought her over to a little dog dish set on a ceramic tray in the corner. "I guess I can see why they could only afford to Cancun," she said quietly to Lisa, who pulled out a kitchen chair and sat down. "Look at this kitchen! These cabinets have to be custom made, and I don't even know where you'd get appliances like that."

"They look industrial to me," Lisa agreed, eyeing the stainless-steel behemoths. "I guess she was pretty privileged."

When Maggie was done, Courtney sat down at the table. The dog had taken a liking to her, apparently, because she lay down right across the tops of Courtney's sneakers. "It even smells like fresh paint in here. Who could possibly afford to do so much remodeling all at once? If I ever do find a house—because I don't think I want the one next door anymore—then I'll probably just make it mine one gallon of paint at a time. I'd have to take out a second mortgage to do things so extensive." Even though she couldn't quite fathom the wealth of some people, Courtney still enjoyed looking at it. The deep cherry stain on the cabinets was pleasant to look at, and someone had made the raised panels in the door match the curve on the arched interior doorways of the home. This place had charm, for sure.

Detective Fletcher's voice floated out of the next room. "Mr. DuBois, I understand they explained to you over the phone that your wife is deceased."

"Yes, sir." The responding voice was quiet, barely above a whisper.

"We have yet to determine the cause, but we like to have all the information we can to be as thorough as possible. Mrs. DuBois was likely out there since sometime last night. Had the two of you spoken?"

"Not for a couple of days, actually. We hadn't been getting along very well, and we were taking some time apart." Mr. DuBois cleared his throat. "I hadn't been staying here at night."

Hearing this, Courtney sat up straight and looked at Lisa. That didn't seem quite right to her. Maggie was snoring away on top of her shoes, making it a little harder to hear.

"I understand," Fletcher replied. "And can you tell me where you were last night?"

"Sure. I went to the trivia night fundraiser for the Curly Bay Pirates with my buddy Zach Young. The high school band is trying to get new instruments."

"Right. I heard about that. Mr. DuBois, I'm sure there are going to be several more times that we'll be in contact with you due to the nature of this. Now, about that other matter we spoke about earlier..." Fletcher trailed off.

Courtney leaned slightly toward the doorway, desperate to know exactly what that meant.

"I don't want it," Mr. DuBois said, sounding more firm than he had about anything else Courtney had overheard.

"Then I'll let you step into the kitchen and handle it yourself."

Quickly pretending she hadn't been listening, Courtney prepared herself to feign surprise when the two men entered the kitchen. She didn't have to pretend at all when she saw Mr. DuBois. The dark-haired man with narrow shoulders and glasses was definitely not the same person Raquel had been having lunch with at Salazar's Salad Bar. Fortunately, given the situation, Courtney didn't think it would be all that odd for her to act nervous. "Hi, there. I'm Courtney," she said as she held out her hand. "I'd stand up, but I'm afraid Maggie's had a tough afternoon." She glanced down, where the terrier was still snoring away happily.

"Aaron DuBois." He shook her hand as he introduced himself, his expression troubled as he eyed the dog. "Look, um, Detective Fletcher said you run a shelter?"

"I do. I'm the manager at the Curly Bay Pet Hotel and Rescue." She didn't bother telling him that Raquel had come by looking to board Maggie, since she had a good feeling he didn't even know she was going on vacation.

"That's great. Uh, I hate to ask you this, but could you take the dog? She was Raquel's, not mine, and I really don't know what to do with her."

Courtney felt her mouth fall open, but she quickly snapped it shut again after a glance at Detective Fletcher. Somehow, Courtney hadn't imagined that Maggie was probably a more recent acquisition, just like the swimming pool and new kitchen. "I can do that. There's a little bit of paperwork to do if you'd like to sign her over to us."

He glanced down at the dog, whose lips were flapping gently with every snore. "I think it'd be for the best."

"I'll get what I need out of the car."

Fifteen minutes later, Aaron was locking up the house as Courtney loaded Maggie into the back of her car. Fletcher hovered on the sidewalk, and he touched her elbow when she turned around. His eyes were serious, though she'd rarely seen them otherwise. "Do me a favor and keep your eyes open, huh?"

"Right."

Courtney dropped off Lisa and headed for the shelter with Maggie in the passenger seat. "I'm really sorry, little girl. You've had a rough day, and you deserve to be in a comfortable home with someone. You probably won't like being in a cage, but I promise you it won't be as bad as you think."

Maggie sat with her back legs splayed out on either side of her, watching Courtney talk.

"You're cute, though. I'd gamble you're purebred, given Raquel's other tastes. Someone will snap you up quick, and you'll be back in the lap of luxury before you know it."

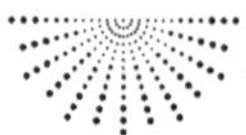

CHAPTER SIX

"How's Maggie doing?" Courtney asked Dora on Monday morning. "I put her on this side, since I figured it would be a little quieter, but we can move her over to the shelter if she's doing all right."

Dora smiled at the little dog, whom she was trying to groom. Maggie kept rolling over to have her belly brushed and then biting playfully at the brush. "She's adjusting far better than most of the dogs we get in here on either side. I'm not sure she's really figured out that her owner is gone."

Courtney considered the silly little dog before turning for the door. "Let's hope she doesn't figure it out before she gets a new home, because I'd hate to see another sad pup on our hands."

"I take it that comment is in regard to Peppa?" Dora asked.

Courtney paused. She always thought of Dora as being so busy with the hotel side of things that she didn't really notice the shelter pets who came and went, but then Dora always proved her wrong. "Yeah. She breaks my heart. I know even if I'd committed to a house this weekend it would probably still be another month before I got the keys, and then I'd have to get settled in before I actually brought a foster dog home, but I still feel so guilty about it."

"Something will come along, and in the meantime, we'll just keep doing everything we can," Dora reassured her. "We've seen a lot of sad animals, but you have to admit that most of the time we make them happier than they've ever been before."

Maggie yipped in approval. She'd rolled back over, putting her chin down on the grooming table and her backside in the air as she tried to get Dora to play.

"I guess you're right. Let me know when she's done with her grooming session, and we'll get some pictures for the website." Courtney had made it her mission when she'd come to the shelter to do as much with their marketing as possible. She had, after all, been in the advertising business for quite some time when she lived in the city, and if she used those skills then it didn't all have to go to waste. The advertising budget wasn't very extensive, so most of her efforts included spending a lot of time on their social media sites and getting out in the community to spread the word.

Coming back through the office on the way to the shelter, Courtney found Jessi in the office. She sat in her desk chair with her back to the door, hunched over as she pressed her cell to her ear.

"Yeah, we could probably do that." There was a long pause. "Sure, but I've got to work the next day so I can't stay out too late." Jessi let out a sigh as she set her elbow down on her desk with a thunk. "Sorry, but I take my job seriously. There are a lot of animals depending on me."

Courtney did her best to go about her work. There was always a mountain of paperwork to do, no matter how hard she tried to streamline things and get them online. The house and Raquel's death were distracting enough as she went through the vet bills and the checking account, but Jessi's conversation was even harder to ignore.

"Yes," she hissed, "I do want to go out with you. Just because I have a life outside of you doesn't mean it's all right for you to make me feel guilty when I have other things to do. Yeah. Yeah, I'm sorry too. All right. I'll talk to you later."

Courtney pursed her lips, watching as Jessi tossed the phone on her desk and shoved herself out of her chair. She stomped out of the room toward the shelter, letting the door shut hard behind her. It was difficult as a manager to decide when she should try to get involved in her employees' personal lives. As a rule, Courtney figured it wasn't her problem as long as the work was getting done. Clearly, though, there was something really wrong.

"Hey," she said gently as she stepped into the rescue, finding Jessi holding a fluffy white cat they'd dubbed Coconut. "Is everything all right? You seemed upset."

Jessi shook her head and scratched Coconut behind the ears. "Yeah, everything's fine. I'm just being dramatic. I'm sorry."

"You don't have to be sorry. I'm just concerned." Courtney bit her tongue against saying anything about how much time Jessi was spending on personal phone calls, but she knew she wouldn't be able to hold back for long.

"I appreciate it. Hey, I made a little bit of progress with Peppa. Do you want to see?" Jessi was smiling, though Courtney noted the smile didn't quite reach her eyes.

"Of course." Dogs were great therapy, and sometimes the ones who needed therapy themselves were the most helpful.

After Jessi put Coconut back in her cage, they went into the kennel. At seeing them, Peppa immediately skittered to the back of her cage as usual. "It takes a minute," Jessi explained, "but I do think it's been helpful." She opened the door and walked just inside, speaking softly all the while. Jessi didn't offer treats or attempt to coax the dog out of the corner. She simply sat down near the front of the cage with her hands folded on her lap.

Courtney stayed as far back as possible so she wouldn't interfere as she watched. At first, nothing happened. Peppa stayed with her back to Jessi and her nose in the corner. After about a minute, she began giving Jessi sidelong glances over her shoulder. Once she realized the human intruder wasn't moving. She turned around and curled up on her bed.

After about five minutes, Jessi got up and came out. "See? I thought it would be good for her not to feel like she has to be pressured into anything every time a person comes around." Now that light had returned to Jessi's eyes, and Courtney knew they'd benefitted each other.

"That's great! Oh." She heard the bell over the front door. "Sounds like I've got to go, but I'll leave you to it."

The man had light brown hair and a wide build, but he had a very calm voice that was familiar somehow. "Hi. I'm looking for a dog."

"We've got plenty of them. Some of them are in foster homes at the moment, so we may have to make an appointment depending on what you're looking for. I've got a little bit of time if you'd like to tour the kennel, though." She moved to let him behind the counter.

He held up a hand. "Ah, actually there's a specific dog I'm looking for, and I don't know if you have her or not. I already checked the pound, though, and she's not there. She's a Boston terrier, and her name is Maggie. At least, it was. I know sometimes shelters rename them."

Courtney felt her heart thudding in her throat. Maggie's owner was dead, and Raquel's husband didn't want her. Who else would? "May I ask how you know Maggie?"

"Sure," he said with a nod, glancing over his shoulder to make sure nobody else was in the lobby. "My name is Jordan Chamness. Maggie was my girlfriend's dog, but she passed away recently."

"I see." This confirmed the suspicion that had been building in Courtney's mind, causing her thoughts to swirl quickly. Jordan must have been the man Raquel was with at Salazar's. Did Aaron DuBois know his wife was cheating? Is that why they hadn't been staying together? She needed more time. "I can tell you that we do have Maggie here, but there is an application process."

"That's not a problem. Whatever it takes."

"I'll get you started on the paperwork." Courtney kept several clipboards loaded up with everything they needed right at the counter, and she handed him one.

Jordan skimmed down the page and paused. "Um, it says I need a vet reference."

"That's correct."

He swallowed, his breath coming in shallow. "I don't have a vet. I haven't had a pet since I was a kid. I really do want to take Maggie home with me, though. She's a sweet little thing, and she deserves to be in a home instead of a shelter. No offense to you and your place, of course."

"None taken." Detective Fletcher had told her to keep her eyes open, and to her that meant he didn't think Raquel's death was necessarily an accident. He wasn't going to tell her that outright, because that would undoubtedly violate some police department rule, but he'd told her, nevertheless. Jordan seemed nice enough, but could he have killed Raquel? "Why don't I fetch Maggie and we can sit down and talk about it?"

"Sounds great."

He'd already finished half the paperwork when Courtney returned with the dog. She opened the gate, watching Maggie carefully. She thoroughly bought into the theory that dogs could tell you a lot about a person if you only knew how to listen.

Maggie told her a lot in a fraction of a second. The Boston was already excited, simply because that was her personality, but she was on the moon as soon as she saw Jordan sitting in the lobby. She scrambled so fast that she lost traction on the linoleum, and when she made it to Jordan she was panting with glee as she tried to climb onto his lap.

"Hey, sweetie! Oh, baby, I'm happy to see you, too!" Jordan's eyes glistened as he scooped up the little dog and let her lick him all over his face and neck. "Have you been a good girl? I'll bet you have! You're the sweetest, aren't you?"

It was the kind of reunion that made Courtney want to cry, but she needed to get down to the heart of the matter. "It looks like the two of you have quite a bond."

"You could say that." Jordan smiled as he pressed kisses all over the dog's face. "You see, Maggie was Raquel's—that was my girlfriend—she was supposed to be Raquel's dog. They liked each other, but I ended up watching Maggie a lot when Raquel was working or busy. We were just crazy about each other, and I can't stand the thought of not having her now that Raquel is gone." A single tear trickled down his cheek, and he wiped it away quickly.

Courtney pretended not to notice, but it was impossible not to see how much these two meant to each other. "Can I ask what happened?" she said gently, gambling on Jordan not knowing she was the one who had found Raquel's body.

"I don't know yet, to be honest. It was really recent, and it's hard to talk about." Jordan buried his face in Maggie's short fur, and she tucked her head into the crook of his neck.

"As far as a vet, the shelter uses Dr. Moulton over on Campbell Street. That would be a good start, and she always gives a discount for the dogs and cats who've been adopted. I can give you her card." Though Courtney knew there was something fishy surrounding Raquel's death, she had an idea now that it wasn't Jordan. The man must have truly cared for her to put up with her rudeness and still grieve for her like that. He was a big guy, the kind who looked more likely to be out playing football than crying into the fur of a little dog, but he and Maggie were obviously close.

"That would be wonderful. Thank you so much. Does that mean I can take her home?"

"We've just got to get the paperwork finished and take care of the fee, and then you'll be good to go." She smiled, choking back her own tears. Courtney had lost out on a house she wanted, and Raquel had lost her life, but at least Maggie was about to go to a good home.

"What do you think, Mags?" Jordan asked as he pressed his face against hers. "You want to go home with me? And we can go jogging in the park? Yeah? That sound good?"

Though she hadn't started an official suspect list, Courtney knew Jordan was firmly crossed off of it.

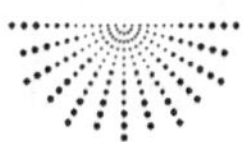

CHAPTER SEVEN

"I'm really glad you had time for lunch today," Courtney said as she got in the passenger seat of Lisa's SUV. "I just can't stop thinking about Raquel DuBois."

"Tell me about it," her friend said with a frown. "It's kind of haunting, and I've been dying to tell everyone I know. That would be horrible, though, so I feel like I have to keep it to myself."

Courtney fiddled with her purse thoughtfully. "It occurred to me that Detective Fletcher wanted us to overhear that conversation with Aaron DuBois."

Lisa kept her eyes on the road, but a slow smile took over her face. "To be honest, I was kind of thinking the same thing. I couldn't imagine a seasoned man like him making a mistake like that. I don't think it was *us,* though. I think it was you, especially since he also asked you to keep your eyes open. I think Fletcher knows just how much of a help you've been."

"Maybe so, but I'm not sure what to do about this. Obviously, since Raquel was having lunch with someone other than her husband, I thought Aaron DuBois would be the prime suspect. You heard him, though. He's got a solid alibi."

"Which leaves the boyfriend!" Lisa concluded.

"It *did,* until he came into the shelter and asked to take Maggie home," Courtney replied.

"What? Don't tell me that when I'm driving! You've got to be kidding me!" Lisa was getting excited, bouncing up and down in her seat. "Tell me what happened."

Courtney did, and she didn't leave out a single detail. "After all that emotion, Jordan Chamness is either an excellent actor or he's genuinely grieving for Raquel."

"Is it impossible for the killer to grieve?" Lisa asked, one eyebrow raised as she pulled into the parking lot in front of Salazar's.

"No, I suppose not. Call it a gut feeling. Besides, we heard the two of them talking when they were here in the restaurant. Raquel was being really nasty to Jordan, and all he did was console her and treat her like some wounded bird that needed help. I think he's just a big sucker. In a good way, mostly." It was certainly a good thing when it came to Jordan's love for Maggie, who was undoubtedly living high on the hog now that her biggest fan had taken her home. It might not have been so great for him when it came to his relationship with Raquel, however.

"Okay. So we can cross off both the husband and the boyfriend. Who's next on the list?" Lisa asked as they got out of the car.

"I don't know. I only knew her from my brief encounter with her at the shelter. I'll have to do some research to see where to look next. It's been keeping me up at night, though. Well, that and Peppa." The little progress that Jessi had made with the beagle mix was wonderful, but it was also extremely slow. That was the nature of things when a scared dog was living in the shelter, but that meant it was only going to continue to be slow until Peppa had a different place to live.

They ordered and fetched their salads, each of them thoughtful as they sat back down at the table. "You should come by the library sometime," Lisa said when she'd had a few bites of her salad. "Maybe we could look her up. I know you can do a lot from home, but we have access to all the newspapers and everything. Plus, it could be fun." She gave her friend a conspiratorial smile over the table.

"I agree. We should do that, but in the meantime, I think there might be another interesting person we can talk to." Courtney pointed across the dining room with her fork, where a familiar waitress was taking an order for a couple with two small children.

"Do you really think a waitress would stalk someone at their home and kill them over a bowl of soup?" Lisa asked.

"Well, I don't know. Sometimes people really lose their tempers, or maybe there have been a lot of little things that keep building up. It happens, I'm sure." She watched the waitress for a little bit longer as she ate, trying to figure out how she was going to talk to her.

That was the problem. She could talk to anyone she wanted about the shelter or the weather or how good the bread rolls were that day, but it wasn't easy to just walk up to a person and ask if they'd killed anyone lately.

"You're going to do it, aren't you?" Lisa asked with a smile.

"Oh, yeah. There's clearly something happening here, and whether the police are talking about it publicly or not, I want to know. I guess I'm more of a busybody than I tend to think." She waited until the waitress was facing the right direction and lifted her hand to signal her.

"Is there something I can get for you?" She asked sweetly as she walked over.

Courtney noted her nametag said Marissa. "I actually just wanted to say we were in here when that woman gave you such a hard time over the squash soup a few days ago. I thought she was really out of line, and it's not fair that you work so hard and then have someone treat you that way."

Marissa sighed and scratched her forehead with her thumbnail. "I appreciate it. That's just the way things go sometimes. I've known Raquel for a long time, though, and I've come to expect that from her."

"Oh, really?" This was a revelation Courtney hadn't expected. "I thought she was just another rude customer."

The waitress glanced over her shoulder to check the status of the dining room, but it wasn't very busy. "Unfortunately, no. We actually went to high school together. Back then, she went by Rachel. She was really sweet and simple, the kind of person who always helped the new kid find their locker and volunteered after school."

"Wow." Courtney was floored. There was nothing about Raquel that fit that description. Even the clothing she'd worn and the way she put on her makeup had been on the harsh side, like she'd wanted the whole world to think she had pointy edges. "I guess she was having a bad day."

"More like a bad year. Something had changed in Rachel recently. I think she saw how many wealthy people there are living in this town, and she decided she wasn't content to just be a normal person anymore. Her husband has kind of a dead-end job, and even though it'd always sounded to me like they were doing pretty well, she wanted more. You hear a lot of people talking when you work in a place like this. Rachel was running them into the ground financially with all these extravagant clothes and home improvements. Then she started seeing that other guy." Marissa rolled her eyes. "He was really sweet, and I felt sorry for him. I knew Rachel was just using him because she wanted her husband to file for divorce. She wasn't going to do it herself, because then she wouldn't have as much chance to get alimony. That part I know is true, because she told me one day when she came in alone."

"That seems like a lot of trouble to go through just to change your image," Courtney remarked.

"I blame social media," Marissa replied honestly as she leaned one hand on the back of the booth. "There are a couple of other girls in our class who make it seem like they really made it big. I don't know if it's true or not, because I tend to doubt anything I see on the internet, but I think maybe Rachel thought she'd missed the boat and hadn't made anything of herself. Our ten-year reunion is coming up. Anyway, I shouldn't be talking about all this. I heard a rumor she passed away. It's just been on my mind a lot, and I tend to talk too much. That's what my boss says, anyway."

"I don't mind," Courtney replied honestly.

Marissa headed off toward the kitchen.

"That was informative," Lisa remarked as she blew on her soup. "Do you think she was being honest?"

"I do. She told us a lot more than I expected. I thought we'd just get a snarky comment about how rude Raquel was and that's it, but we got half her life story. Interesting."

"Interesting? Does that mean the waitress is off your list?"

Courtney studied the kitchen door as she thought. "Marissa went to school with her, and Curly Bay isn't a huge town. She knew about Raquel's personal life and had even talked to her a few times about it, so it's reasonable that Marissa might have known where Raquel lived. I think she had the opportunity, but not the motive."

"Now you're starting to sound like one of those old detective movies." Lisa put down her spoon and used her best old-timey voice. "I knew the dame wasn't the crook, but she wasn't squeaky-clean, either."

The two of them had a fit of giggles over the joke. "That's good inspiration," Courtney said as she wiped tears from her eyes. "I'll have to go home and find some of those crime dramas, and maybe go find a trench coat at Goodwill."

"Does that mean I get to be your lovely assistant? I can answer the phone in a cutesy accent and tell everyone that you're out at the bar drinking?"

They laughed again, and Courtney was so grateful
for Lisa. She had a good friend who could keep her
down-to-earth when she needed to be, but who was
also good at getting her mind off the drama at hand.
"I couldn't think of anyone better."

CHAPTER EIGHT

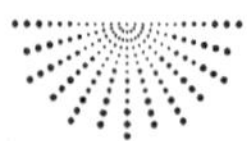

"So the waitress definitely knew something about the victim. For all I know, they'd been really good friends at one point. That's something I didn't think about at the moment. Marissa only said they knew each other in high school, but what if there was more of a rivalry between them? Like Raquel stole Marissa's boyfriend, and then ten years down the line Marissa realized how much that had messed up her life? There's just too much to think about, and I haven't had a chance to find any more information on Raquel. What do you think?"

Peppa didn't respond, only watching quietly from her corner. At least she didn't have her back turned.

"Yeah, I thought so." Courtney thought Jessi's progress with Peppa was a good start, and she was determined for it to keep going. It made sense to her to get the dog used to not only having someone sitting nearby but talking. It didn't matter what the subject was. She just needed as much exposure to people as possible without getting overwhelmed. So far, the dog didn't seem to mind.

"You're a pretty good listener, you know?" Courtney said with a smile. "Just sitting there, staring at me with those big brown eyes like you really care. You don't quite know what to think of me, but you still look like you're concerned. I appreciate it more than you know. This death has really been on my mind lately. It shouldn't be my problem. I happened to be in the wrong place at the wrong time, although that happens a lot. Still, I'm not on the police department. I've got a job to do here, and that shouldn't have anything to do with a potential murder investigation. I just want to help animals, and I guess sometimes that extends out to helping people."

It was just the barest movement, but Courtney swore she saw the very tip of Peppa's tail wag.

"I think you like being talked to," Courtney praised. "We just need to find you someone chatty who's willing to take the time to be patient with you. Your looks aren't a problem at all, you know. With that cinnamon brown fur, a little bit of black around your face and down your back, and then those cute white paws, I think we would've already found you a place if you were just a little more comfortable around people."

Peppa gave another wag of her tail. This time it was a slightly bigger movement.

The dog wasn't exactly jumping in her lap and licking her face like Maggie had done to Jordan, but it still made Courtney feel the same way. "I suppose we should end on a good note, huh?"

She looked up as the door to the kennel opened and Carolyn Davis walked in. "I've heard of method acting, but I didn't know the same thing applied to shelter managers. Do you have to become one with the dog in order to take care of it?" she joked.

"Something like that, in this case." Courtney left a treat on the floor for whenever Peppa was ready for it, and then she stood and came out of the cage. "This poor girl is incredibly shy, so we've been working with her a bit every day."

Carolyn frowned at the gangly pup. "I told you when we first met that I wasn't much of a dog person, and that's true. I still feel so sorry for any of them that are stuck in a situation like this. Just because I don't want them jumping all over my couches doesn't mean I don't care."

Courtney tilted her head as she studied the realtor, wondering where this was coming from. "Of course not."

Her gaze remained on Peppa. "I've been feeling a little bad since we started working on your home search. You came to me because Gunner needed a home. I had a lot of good reasons for not taking him in, not the least of which is how much I'm gone. A dog would be miserable under my care, because I'd never be around. Still, I feel bad and I know how much these animals mean to you. I hope you can forgive me for that."

"Oh, Carolyn!" Courtney couldn't help herself, and she gave the realtor a hug. "There's nothing to forgive! Gunner was a former police dog. That's not the kind of animal you can put in just any home, and I'd much rather that someone be honest about their limitations. We actually found a great place for him, where he's getting all the training he needs. His new owner even told me he gets to sleep on the bed, so you don't have anything to worry about."

"Thank goodness." Carolyn's shoulders slumped with relief. "I'd told myself he was fine, but once you and I started talking again I couldn't get him off my mind. That makes me feel so good."

"I'm glad. Is that why you came down here?" Courtney made sure the latch was in place on Peppa's cage.

"No," Carolyn admitted, "but it seemed like a chance to get that off my shoulders. I actually was in the neighborhood and thought I'd check in about that house you were interested in."

Courtney led the way into the cat room to check on the tenants in there as she tried to explain the situation to Carolyn. "So, as I'm sure you can tell, I'm not too keen on moving right next door to the place where I found a dead body."

The realtor frowned deeply, showing several creases in her forehead. This was a completely different look than she'd had when she was so happily showing the homes. "That is a shame, and it's such a cute house. You know, though, you're going to find a few flaws with every home you look at. It might be neighbors who fight or a tree that constantly drops trees in your yard, but that's just part of being a homeowner." She forced a smile.

"I suppose that's true," Courtney said slowly as she noticed how late it had already gotten in the day. The cats were supposed to have a meal, but their dishes were empty. Where was Jessi?

Carolyn peeked into a cage and tapped her fingers against the wires to get the attention of the little tabby inside. She petted it through the cage as she spoke. "You said you were checking out the neighborhood. Did you by chance go across the street and talk to the Andersons? I sold them their home quite a few years ago, when I was first getting into the business. We still exchange Christmas cards every year, and they tell me how wonderfully that house has worked out for them. They've raised a couple of kids there who are nearly out of high school now. They were just little bitty things when the Andersons bought their home."

"I didn't," Courtney said cautiously as she headed for the food bin in the corner. "I remembered you saying that, but I wanted to feel everything out for myself. You know, to really be sure this was the home I wanted. I didn't expect all that with Raquel DuBois to happen, and even though the area seems nice, I'm not sure I could ever completely forget that."

"Is there something I can do to help you with that?" Carolyn asked as she gestured toward the cat food.

Courtney eyed the cream outfit the realtor wore, thinking that Carolyn definitely hadn't come dressed to work in a shelter. "You could open and close the cage doors for me. That would save me some time. We start right here at this corner and work through row by row."

Carolyn eagerly complied as she opened the cage with the tabby in it. "You just let me know if you need to see any of the homes again. I'm happy to help in any way possible. And don't let some little crazy incident get you down. You know, I once had a client fall down the stairs when he came to look at a home because the railing was loose. I was horrified, but he took it as a sign that he was supposed to have the place. He was good with his hands, and he liked the idea of fixing it up."

"That's nice, but I'm not sure I want to stay in the habit of finding corpses," Courtney noted as they moved on to a cage shared by two orange and white cats who'd come in together as siblings. She was starting to wonder why Carolyn was so desperate all of a sudden. Could the realtor have known about Raquel and Aaron's marital problems and decided to take matters into her own hands so she wouldn't lose out on a commission?

The realtor's fingers shook slightly as she opened the door so Courtney could feed a fat calico. "I'm sorry. I don't mean to be pushy. It's just that this time of year is supposed to be a little busier than it has been. I've still sold several houses this month, but as you saw there are only so many homes in Curly Bay. I get worried when the trends don't hold."

Courtney let go of a knot of tension in her shoulders that she hadn't realized was there until that moment. "I understand. Don't worry. I do plan to buy a house. There are too many reasons for me to get out of that apartment, even though my landlord tried to tell me I should stay. I just have to find the right place. Like you said, I really need to connect to it."

"You're right. You're so right, and I've let my own needs get in the way of that. I'm really sorry. I'll do better." Carolyn had always been the epitome of professionalism, and to see her drop that façade was a stark change.

"It's all right. Really. I know how it is to be passionate about something, and it only makes it more complicated when that passion happens to be your job as well. You find yourself pushing the cause, and it's impossible not to. I do it all the time." Courtney gave the calico a scratch under the chin before they moved to the next cage.

"I know exactly what you mean! I was a at a trivia fundraiser for the Pirates a few nights ago. I was just there because my nephew is in the band and I want to support the community as much as possible, but I found myself giving out cards to everyone I encountered, just in case they might want a house at any point in the future. It's kind of ridiculous when you think about it." Carolyn laughed as she tucked her hair behind her ear.

Courtney's ears perked up. That trivia night fundraiser was the same one Aaron DuBois had mentioned as his alibi for the night Raquel died. Good. Courtney didn't want to believe that the realtor had done anything too extreme just for the sake of a sale. She liked Carolyn.

"We can go down to the next row now, so that white cat down there is next." Courtney gestured to the next feline in line.

As soon as the cage door was opened, Coconut stepped to the front of the cage. She rubbed her head against the doorway, gazing sweetly up at Carolyn while giving a trill of a meow.

"Oh, hello to you, too! Aren't you just the prettiest thing?" Carolyn bent down to let the cat sniff her hand, but Coconut didn't want to waste any time. She bumped her head up against the bottom of the realtor's hand and marched across the front of the cage to extend the pet all the way down her back. "Is she always this sweet?"

Courtney smiled. When she'd first come to the Curly Bay Pet Hotel and Rescue, she'd thought finding a home for a pet was simply a matter of logic. The person needed to have room in their home and in their life, and the dog or cat needed to be comfortable with the kind of lifestyle of the family that was adopting it. Now, she knew it was so much more than that. "No, not really. Not that she's ever been disagreeable, but that's still more than I usually see from her. Just like you said about houses, a person and a pet need to have a special kind of connection."

Coconut apparently agreed, because she was completely ignoring the cat chow in her dish in favor of Carolyn. She squeezed her big green eyes slowly in admiration, which was the feline way of saying she liked someone.

"You can pick her up, if you'd like." Courtney wasn't sure Carolyn would want to, given her nice outfit, but the realtor surprised her by taking her up on her offer immediately.

"Hello, darling," Carolyn cooed. "How is such a pretty, delicate thing like you in a shelter? This is no place for you." She looked up at Courtney, joy evident in her face. "Can you tell me a little bit about her?"

"She was taken in as a stray, and nobody claimed her. We don't really know much else about her, but I've got a feeling she's used to living in the lap of luxury. The poor thing was gray instead of white when she was brought in, but she's never been upset about baths or grooming. She's quite the little lady."

"I can see that." Carolyn's smile grew wider as Coconut butted her head against the realtor's shoulder and meowed sweetly. "Courtney?"

"Yes?"

"I think I'm in love."

"I think she is, too." It was so wonderful to see this, and Courtney understood on an even deeper level what Carolyn had meant when she said she liked to see her clients get the home that was right for them.

Sometimes it was a fixer-upper, like a dog who still needed a lot of work and training. Sometimes it was a home that was fresh and new and clean, like Coconut. Either way, there was no better reward than seeing it all come together the way it was meant to be. "If you're interested in her, we could do the paperwork once I finish feeding the rest of the cats."

"Oh, right!" Carolyn blinked, suddenly remembering that the real world was still happening around her no matter how intriguing the cat was. She put Coconut back her cage. "You stay right there," she said wistfully. "I'm going to help the other kitties, and then I'll come back and get you."

"I take that as a yes?" Courtney asked with a smile as they distributed another scoop of food to the next cage.

"You really drive a hard bargain, but I guess I'll take her off your hands," Carolyn joked.

They finished with the feeding, and Courtney brought Carolyn up to the front to get started on the forms. That made two animals this week that were getting new homes. Maggie had only had to stay at the shelter for a very short time, and Coconut had been there several months, but they were both going to the places they were meant to be.

The feeling of hope and love in Courtney's chest deflated a little as she realized she still hadn't seen Jessi. "I'll be right back." She double-checked the kennel on the shelter side, but nobody was there. Popping over to the hotel, she found Dora up to her elbows in Collie fur. "Have you seen Jessi?"

Dora wiped her face against her sleeve as she combed out the massive amounts of fluff. "I can't say that I have. I'm not sure I've seen her since first thing this morning, actually, but my grooming schedule has been pretty busy today. I've been cutting and combing since I got here."

"Okay. Do you need any help? I've got someone doing papers up front, but I've got a few minutes." Courtney knew that Jessi and Dora were always good at keeping up with their respective sides of the business, but she was always happy to jump in and help wherever she was needed.

"No, I'm fine for now. Just do me a favor and don't agree to any walk-ins today."

"Can do." Courtney peeked in the office once again, and then she checked her watch. It wasn't time for Jessi's break yet, so where could she be? On a gamble, Courtney peeked out the back door.

Jessi's back was to her, her cell phone pressed against her ear once again as she leaned against the side of the building. "Yeah, I miss you, too. I know. Well, if you're working on Thursday night, then maybe we could get together on Friday. Sure. That would be nice."

Courtney stood there for a moment, trying to decide what to do. If she was still at Miller and Martinez, the advertising company she'd worked for in the city, anyone who was caught taking a personal phone call would be immediately reprimanded. It was a different matter when there were only three people who all had to work in the same building and never see anyone different. Still, Courtney was the manager. She couldn't just let that go. She cleared her throat.

Jessi whipped around, her brows drawn together angrily at first until she saw who it was. Then her face paled. "I've got to go. I'll talk to you later." She hung up and stuffed her phone in her pocket. "Sorry. I guess I was out here a little longer than I meant to be. I just got caught up in…" She gestured helplessly toward her phone.

"That's fine, but I really need you back in there. I already gave the cats their meal, but I've got a customer that I need to get back to." As a realtor who was used to filling out forms, Carolyn probably wouldn't take long to finish, and Courtney didn't want to keep her waiting.

"Sure. No problem. I'll get right on the dogs' post-lunch walk." Jessi jogged into the building.

Courtney followed her, knowing she'd have to get this taken care of soon enough.

CHAPTER NINE

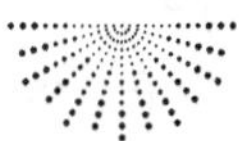

The next day, Courtney sat in her office scrolling through the realty site on the computer and talking to her mother on her lunch break.

"I thought you said you looked at pretty much everything that was available when you went out with the realtor," Mrs. Cain observed when her daughter told her what she was up to. "I doubt anything is just going to pop up over the course of a few days. I've been reading a lot about the housing market, and it sounds like it's pretty stable right now."

"Why were you reading about that?" Courtney asked. Her parents had been living in the same house for over forty years, and she couldn't imagine them moving now.

"Because you said you wanted to move," her mother replied simply. "We might not get to live near each other, but I still like to be involved. It's good to know a thing or two about what's happening in the world, too, and not just your little corner of it. Have you checked out the current mortgage interest rates?"

Courtney shook her head and smiled. Her mother was always busy, but Courtney usually heard this through the phone as the sound of pots and pans rattling or her mother breathing heavily as she worked in the garden. Apparently, her busy nature included research on the internet as well. "I have, and I've also talked to my bank. I won't have any problem getting a loan."

"I'm not surprised," her mother gushed. "You were always good with your money. I remember when you had counted up all the coins in your piggy bank and came to me asking to open a savings account. I was so proud of you, and it's nice to know you still hold onto your pennies."

"When I need to, I do. I just want to make sure I spend them on the right thing, and this house I was considering isn't it." Courtney had decided not to reveal all the details about Raquel's death to her mom, just so she wouldn't worry. "I could very well spend the rest of my life in whatever house I buy, and I don't want to be unhappy with it."

"That's all very sound logic, but keep in mind that nothing is going to be perfect. You know, when your father insisted that we buy this house, I was a little upset about it. I didn't think it was big enough. That was the main thing. Now that you're all grown up and moved out, though, I'm happy we don't have a larger space to take care of. This is perfect for us, and you'll find one that's perfect for you. You just might not know it yet."

"Thanks. I'm going to keep my eyes open and remind myself that there's not really a rush. I want to foster some dogs, but in the meantime at least I have a roof over my head."

A bright ding sounded on the other end of the phone. "Oh, that's my cue to punch down the bread dough."

"I'll let you go. I've got to get back to work. I love you, Mom."

"I love you, too. Invite us down when you get settled into a place!"

Hanging up, Courtney jumped when she heard the door to the hotel slam. Jessi came storming through the office and out the other side to the shelter, where she slammed that door behind her as well. Before a baffled Courtney could follow her, Dora showed up.

"You need to have a talk with that girl, because you wouldn't be pleased if I did it," Dora advised.

"What happened?" Courtney had never heard the two of them fight before.

Dora put one fist on her hip. "She demanded that I stop what I was doing to groom one of the cats. I told her it would have to wait because I was still working on appointments. That's how we've always done it unless there's an emergency."

Courtney nodded. Just a few months ago, she never would've known what constituted a grooming 'emergency.' After seeing a dog come in from Animal Control with knots so bad they kept him from walking properly, she now knew. "That's right."

"I wasn't rude, but she accused me of caring more about the pampered pups over here than the animals who really need me, and she stormed out. I don't know what to think!" Dora flipped her free hand in the air, clearly frazzled.

She'd been putting it off for far too long, and Courtney realized she'd let a small problem build into a bigger one. "Don't worry about it. You take care of what you need to, and I'll handle it."

"Thanks."

Courtney found Jessi sitting in Peppa's cage. "Hey. Let's you and I go out to dinner tonight."

Jessi kept her gaze on the dog. "No, thanks. I don't really have time tonight."

Twisting her lips together, Courtney looked for a better way of phrasing things. She didn't like having to get tough, but Jessi wasn't giving her much choice. "It's either we go out and have some dinner, on me, or we take time away from the dogs and cats who need us while we talk about what's going on with you and how it's affecting the business."

Jessi's head fell forward as she twiddled her fingers. "All right. Where should I meet you?"

"How about Russo's Pizza? I can pick you up if you'd like."

Jessi shook her head. "No, that's okay. I'll be there. Does seven work for you?"

"That would be perfect."

It was difficult to wait so long to talk about things, but at least it gave Courtney some time to think about what she was going to say. Jessi had been avoiding her and keeping to herself in general throughout the rest of the workday, and by the time Courtney pulled up to Russo's she was more than ready to have this over with.

The scent of garlic bread was thick in the cool air, even outside. Courtney zipped up her jacket and jogged through the parking lot, thinking she would need to get her actual winter coat out before too long. She stepped inside, grateful for the heat from the kitchens, and got a table.

Jessi showed up just a few minutes later, sliding into the booth as though she were on her way to death row. "Sorry I'm a little late."

"You're fine. I only just got here myself. I went ahead and started on the breadsticks, though. I don't care how many diet plans come out saying we shouldn't have carbs. I'm going to devour them every time."

Jessi smiled as she took one from the basket on the table and nibbled it.

"Feel free to order whatever you'd like. I think I'm going to have a calzone," Courtney said brightly.

The waiter approached, and Jessi ordered spaghetti. "So, what do you want to talk about?"

Apparently, Jessi was dreading this just as much as Courtney was and wanted to be done with it. "I think you already know, but I've noticed you've been really moody lately. It's not my business for the most part, but when it starts to affect everyone else, it is. Dora said the two of you got into an argument today."

"Yeah." Jessi slumped down in the seat. "I shouldn't have snapped at her. I was just frustrated because I felt overwhelmed, and I didn't feel like I had the time to stop and brush the knots out of Peaches. I should've just done it. I'll apologize to her tomorrow."

"I'm sure she'll appreciate that, and so will I, but I'm worried about what's really happening with you. It's not just the argument, you know. You've been taking a ton of personal calls, and they're pulling you away from your actual work. I try to be pretty lenient, since I know we all have things that need to be taken care of every now and then, but it's getting pretty bad."

Jessi let out a long sigh. "I'm sorry. You see, I started seeing this guy named Zach about a month ago. I really like him, and we have a lot of fun together, but he doesn't really hang out with the same kind of crowd that I do."

"Oh?" Courtney had suspected it was about Jessi's dating life based on her phone calls, so she wasn't surprised.

"He's the same age as me, but he still acts like he's in college. He and his friends are always wanting to go out drinking and partying, and they don't care how late they stay out or if they get to work on time the next morning. That's fine for them, I guess, but I do care." Jessi ripped her breadstick into tiny little pieces on her napkin.

Courtney's heart went out to her. "We like to think that our interests and lifestyles really don't matter when it comes to relationships, but I think they do. It makes it a lot harder to get along when you're living such different lives." She had thought she and her former fiancé Sam Smythe had a lot in common when they got together, since they worked for the same company. That hadn't worked out at all.

"It's just so unfair. I'm getting close to thirty, and I don't want to waste my time with someone who might not be right for me. On the other hand, Zach and I have a really good time when we go out together. It's like we've got this connection, but I don't feel it as much when we start having to work around each other's schedules." It was obvious that Jessi was truly miserable as she struggled with this situation.

"Tell me a little about him," Courtney offered, knowing it was good sometimes just to talk even if it wasn't any kind of solution.

"His name is Zach Young, and he works for a finance company. I've seen him when he goes to work, with a button-down shirt and slacks, and it's completely different from the way he looks on the weekends. Actually, I didn't even recognize him the first time I saw him out in public in a hoodie and jeans. His hair is different, and he even carries himself differently. It's kind of weird." Their food arrived and Jessi sprinkled a thick coating of parmesan on top of her pasta.

"Some people are like that, especially if they have to be a little more conservative at work. Wait a second." Courtney's stomach rumbled as the smell of her calzone drifted up, but something much more important than hunger had clicked in her mind. "Did you say Zach Young?"

"Yeah. Do you know him?"

"No, but I think I know someone who does." Courtney hadn't written the name down, but she was fairly certain that was the name Aaron DuBois had given Detective Fletcher for his alibi. "Did you guys go out last Saturday night?"

Jessi nodded. "We've been out together every weekend since we started seeing each other."

"Did you go to the trivia night fundraiser for the high school?" Adrenaline was rushing through Courtney's system now, and she could taste it in her mouth.

"I didn't even know that was happening until I heard a few other people talking about it, or else I might've gone. I was in band in high school. But no, we went over to Ruby Cove where some of his friends were getting together." Jessi twirled her fork in her spaghetti.

"I see. Do you know if Zach has a friend named Aaron?" As hungry as she'd been a moment ago, Courtney's stomach now felt like a brick was sitting in it.

"I think so. Are you sure you don't know him?"

Courtney knew this was too much to explain, and she needed to do something about it. "I'm not sure. Can you excuse me for a minute? I have to make a phone call." Courtney had Detective Fletcher's number pulled up as she stepped out of the restaurant.

CHAPTER TEN

"I admit I was bummed when you passed on that first place, but I think it's going to pay off," Carolyn said from the driver's seat. This time they headed toward the edge of town. Turning onto a gravel lane and then up a long driveway, a little white house slowly revealed itself from among the trees and bushes. Whoever had been living here had taken care of the place, considering the fall flowers that were gently dying back along the front of the house.

"I'm excited to see it. I'm trying not to get my hopes up too much after last time, though. How's Coconut settling in?"

"Oh, she's an absolute doll! She patrols the place when I'm gone, and the neighbors tell me they can see her hanging out in the windows all the time. When I'm home, she's instantly on my lap. I love her!"

"I'm so glad."

They got out of the car, and Carolyn led the way to a spacious living room with a large picture window. "This is a two-bedroom, one-bath house. The kitchen and bathroom have been completely redone. Most of the flooring has already been replaced with linoleum, but you can see there's still carpet in the living room and bedrooms."

There was just something about this house that felt absolutely right to Courtney. Logically, she knew it was good that the kitchen and bath had already been remodeled, because that was work she probably couldn't do on her own. A little bit of paint and flooring here and there weren't a big deal. The linoleum that'd already been laid would be easy to clean, but there was also carpet in case she had a dog in here who had mobility issues and needed more grip. The big windows and the massive yard were a huge plus, as well as the fact that it was far back off the road. Courtney was beginning to enjoy how quiet Curly Bay was compared to the city, and she'd have even more of that experience out here on the edge of town. There were a few neighbors nearby, but it wasn't that crowded. The large, two-car garage had been finished with plywood, and it even had an attic for storage space and its own bathroom. Her heart soared at all the possibilities!

"I'd be crazy not to take this," she gushed when they came back into the living room.

Carolyn raised an eyebrow. "You haven't even asked the price."

"Right. Go ahead and shatter all my hopes and dreams and get it over with." Courtney tensed as she waited, but she let out a squeal of delight when Carolyn gave her the asking price. "I can afford that! I'll take it!"

A month later, Courtney had to hold a very excited Peppa back as the doorbell rang. "Easy there, girl. I know you're excited for company, but you can't be rude." She opened the door to let Lisa and Beau inside.

The border collie and the beagle mix sniffed each other thoroughly before they ran off to play together.

"I'd say they won't have any problem," Lisa said with a smile. "This place is great! I can't wait to see it all."

The doorbell rang again. "Hang on." It was Jessi and Dora, who had made up enough after their fight at the office that they'd decided to ride together.

"We brought you a couple of housewarming gifts," Dora explained. "We weren't sure what you needed, but there are gift receipts if you need them." She handed over two rolled up rugs.

"They're perfect." Courtney gave each of them a hug. "Just small enough that they can fit in the washing machine, and a nice neutral color that won't show dog prints. It's like you know me or something! But you didn't have to bring anything."

"We wanted to," Jessi insisted. "Dora also made you a casserole so you can concentrate on getting moved in the rest of the way." She held out a covered dish.

"You guys are just too much. I didn't mean for this to be any official sort of party. I still have quite a few boxes to unpack and some painting to do before I even invite my parents down." Courtney couldn't wait to show off her new home and to explain how each feature of the house would work well for her.

Beau and Peppa came tearing back into the room, with Beau in the front. He dodged around the back of the couch, hiding. Peppa jumped up on top of the cushions and peered over the back. She barked, and Beau came running back out again, his tongue hanging out in glee.

Lisa laughed. "I guess we'll have to schedule some play dates, which means I can come help you paint while the dogs play. I think Beau will appreciate it, too."

Courtney was just about to give them a tour of the home when Carolyn stopped by. "I just wanted to make sure everything was going well!"

"Absolutely! Come on in so you can see it with furniture." She let in her realtor, who was swiftly becoming one of her friends. Courtney took them through the house, discussing her plans for future foster pups, turning the guest bedroom into an office, and planting shade trees in the backyard. It was too muddy to go outside, since it'd been raining for three days straight, but the spring would bring plenty of time for that.

Courtney was surprised when the doorbell rang once again. "Who could that be? I'm not expecting anyone."

Detective Fletcher stood on her doorstep. "I heard you had a new address," he said as he held out a card. "I thought I'd bring you a little something, as well as some information."

The other women were sitting in the dining room having some cupcakes, so Courtney brought the detective into the kitchen. "I'm listening."

"First, I'm sorry I had to wait so long to tell you this. Aaron DuBois had a really good lawyer, and that made it a little more difficult, but we've finally got everything lined up."

Peppa came dashing into the room, paused long enough to sniff Fletcher's foot and wag her tail, and then went racing out again.

"Anyway," he continued with a smile, "that tip you gave us about Aaron's alibi was spot on. Zach Young was the one who spilled the beans, confessing he'd agreed to lie for Aaron. Neither one of them were at the trivia night fundraiser. Aaron was tired of his wife trying to con a divorce out of him, and he knew she'd take him for every cent he had and would ever earn. He'd moved out, thinking she'd calm down eventually, but she was relentless. He knew her habits, and he took her out."

Courtney shook her head. "Raquel was pretty rude, and she hurt a lot of people, but it's still a shame." She thought about Jordan Chamness and how heartbroken he'd been over Raquel's death. At least, Maggie had a good life, and Jordan would probably be much better off as well.

"Yes, but at least we got to the bottom of it, thanks to you. The department wasn't willing to consider this a homicide, but I had a hunch you were feeling just as suspicious about it as I was. I really do appreciate your help." He tapped the card he'd given her. "You put that to good use. This is a nice little place you have here, and you deserve it."

Before Courtney could protest, Detective Fletcher was making his way to the front door. He gave her a slight smile and a nod—the most enthusiastic thanks she could get from such a melancholy man—and was on his way out.

"What's that?" Jessi asked when Courtney walked back in the dining room.

"Detective Fletcher gave me a card." She sat down and opened it, showing them the gift card to the local home store. "I think that's going to buy plenty of paint, and maybe a few other things, too!"

Lisa lifted her glass. "Welcome home, Courtney!"

THANK YOU FOR CHOOSING A PUREREAD BOOK!

We hope you enjoyed the story, and as a way to thank you for choosing PureRead we'd like to send you this free Special Edition Cozy, and other fun reader rewards…

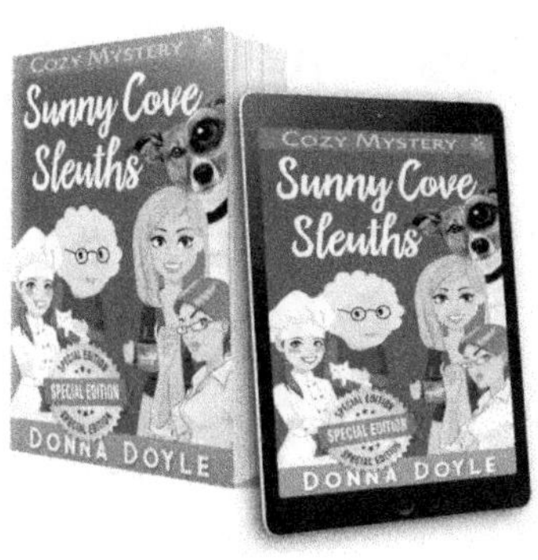

Click Here to download your free Cozy Mystery
PureRead.com/cozy

Thanks again for reading.

See you soon!

The Missing Pom Mystery

The Case of the Confused Canine

A Case Full of Cats

A Furry case of Foul Play

The Case of a Beagle and a Body

A Case of Canines, Cats, & Costumes

A Case of Frauds and Friendly Lizards

A Very Furry Christmas Mystery

The Mysterious Case of Books, Barks, & Burglary

**Also, be sure to get your free copy of Sunny Cove
Sleuths**

PureRead.com/cozy

At PureRead we publish books you can trust. Great tales without smut or swearing, but with all of the mystery and romance you expect from a great story.

Be the first to know when we release new books, take part in our fun competitions, and get surprise free books in your inbox by signing up to our Reader list.

As a thank you you'll receive this exclusive Special Edition Cozy available only to our subscribers...

Click Here to download your free Cozy Mystery
PureRead.com/cozy

Thanks again for reading.
See you soon!